# Me First

## Max Kornell

NANCY PAULSEN BOOKS ◉ AN IMPRINT OF PENGUIN GROUP (USA)

With love for my wife, Erin, who came first,
Psipsina, Ajax, Ramona . . . and Sosie Mae,
who came last—which, it turns out,
is not such a bad place to be!

NANCY PAULSEN BOOKS
Published by the Penguin Group
Penguin Group (USA) LLC
375 Hudson Street, New York, NY 10014

USA | Canada | UK | Ireland | Australia
New Zealand | India | South Africa | China
penguin.com
A Penguin Random House Company

Library of Congress Cataloging-in-Publication Data
Kornell, Max.
Me first / Max Kornell.
pages cm
Summary: A brother and sister's constant attempts to outdo each other land them in a sticky situation.
[1. Brothers and sisters—Fiction. 2. Sibling rivalry—Fiction. 3. Donkeys—Fiction.] I. Title.
PZ7.K83747Me 2014
[E]—dc23
2013024242

Manufactured in China by South China Printing Co. Ltd.
ISBN 978-0-399-15997-8
10 9 8 7 6 5 4 3 2 1

Design by Marikka Tamura.
Text set in HandySans.
The illustrations were drawn and colored with acrylic ink.

Hal was Martha's older brother.
"Did you know," he told Martha,
"that I used to play checkers with
Dad before you were even born?"

Martha didn't mind that Hal was older
or that he talked about it all the time.
It made beating him more fun.
  "Do you know what?" said Hal.
"I let you win."

"I beat Hal at checkers," Martha announced. "He was playing his hardest and I still won."

"No," said Hal. "I *wanted* to lose to see what it felt like."

"Can you two take a break from arguing, please?" Mom asked. "We're going to the river for a picnic, so go pack your things."

Hal and Martha loved the river.
They rushed to get their towels
and swimsuits.

"Look, Hal," said Martha. "My bag is all packed.
Beat you again."
"No," said Hal. "Packing isn't a real race.
I have a better idea . . ."

Hal sprinted out the front door.
"Race you to Gopher's Rock!" he yelled.

Martha trotted to the bottom of the hill.
Hal smiled and said, "Sorry, I win."
But Martha wasn't headed for Gopher's Rock . . .

Instead, she touched the tree stump and said, "I win, too."
"We weren't racing to the stump!" said Hal.
"I was," said Martha.
"Children," Dad said. "I thought we were taking a break from arguing. Let's go."

Hal and Martha tried to take a break from arguing, but when they got to the river, there were too many exciting ways to try to outdo each other.

After lunch, it got cloudy. Mom and Dad decided
it was time to leave. Martha asked if she could take
a new path home.

"Okay," said Mom, "but only if Hal goes with you."

Hal was excited to try the path, too.
"Now," said Hal, "we can both be
the first ones to go this way."
"But it was my idea first,"
said Martha.

Hal and Martha wandered up a hill
and came to a patch of berries.
  "Let's try them," said Martha.
"Me first!"

She popped one into her mouth, then
spit it out. "Yuck! That was horrible!"

Hal saw a big hollow log near the path.
"Let's crawl through it," he said. "Me first!"
He squeezed through and came out covered
in cobwebs. "That was *really* horrible!"
Martha helped him clean up.

Hal and Martha came to the creek.
A tree had fallen and made a bridge.
   "This looks kind of dangerous,"
said Hal.
   But Martha wanted to go first,
and she stepped onto the fallen tree.

There was a terrible cracking sound,
and the log snapped!
Martha fell onto the creek bed below.

Fortunately, Martha wasn't hurt.
But the fall scared her.
     Hal helped her up and they
headed home.

When Hal and Martha got home, neither one was in the mood to outdo the other.

"You had quite a tumble back there. You go ahead," Hal said as he opened the door for Martha.

When it was time to wash up
before dinner, Martha said,
"You wash up first. You're the
one that got covered in cobwebs."

At dinner, Hal offered Martha the mashed potatoes.
Martha poured Hal a glass of milk.

"Hal and Martha," said Mom.
"At dinner, I noticed how thoughtful
you were being with each other.
You really are taking a break from
arguing, and I'm proud of you both."

"You know what?" said Dad. "I noticed that, too, actually, *before* dinner. And I am *very* proud of you."
"Oh, did *you*?" said Mom. "Not that it's a race, but I noticed when they first got home."

"Well, thank you both
for noticing, whenever
you did," said Martha.
"Now we've got a game
to play."

"That's right," said Hal.
"So, who goes first?"